ANNE PERRY

Blood Red Rose

A Timepiece Novel

D1583787

First published in 2012 in Great Britain by
Barrington Stoke Ltd
18 Walker Street, Edinburgh, EH3 7LP

www.barringtonstoke.co.uk

ISBN: 978-1-84299-955-4

Printed in China by Leo

Contents

Chapter 1
Speaking Up

Rosie sat as far back as she could on the café sofa and hoped that Stacey Summers would leave without seeing her. Just a few weeks before, the two girls had been best friends but for the last while they had found they had less and less in common, and now they almost didn't speak at all. Rosie knew that Stacey missed her and wanted to patch things up, but she didn't miss Stacey one bit. The thing was that Stacey and Rosie only got on when Rosie acted up in school and mucked about and got into trouble, and Rosie wasn't interested in doing that any more.

Some funny things had happened to Rosie over the past months, and a few of those things had made her believe in herself a bit more. The fact that Zack Edwards had started to hang out with Rosie had helped with that, since he was by far the hottest boy in school. Zack was coming to meet her here in a few minutes, in fact, and Rosie didn't want Stacey to see the two of them together. Knowing Stacey she'd find a way of spoiling things for Rosie, just out of spite. She had wanted Zack for herself.

After what seemed like a long, long time Stacey chose an iced bun from the display on the counter, paid up and walked out of the shop. Rosie let out her breath and sat up again. She only had time to smooth her hair and put on a bit more lip gloss before Zack arrived.

Stacey and all the other girls in school liked Zack because he was dead good-looking, but Rosie liked him because he was kind. His brother Josh was in the army and Zack worried about him all the time. He was always reading the papers and telling Rosie about the horrible things that happened to people all over the world. Zack said that one day he'd like to work for a charity that helped people in poor countries in Africa and places like that.

Today Zack had a leaflet to show Rosie about people in East Africa starving because the weather was too dry and it was killing their crops and animals. Rosie wasn't good at reading and even though she was getting some help from a group in the local library, she still couldn't make out what the leaflet said. No way was she ready to tell Zack about her little problem, so instead she tried to ask questions that she hoped were clever.

"My dad says all the money we give to these countries gets stolen," she said. "He says the people who run things take it to buy cars and stuff and so it never gets given to the people who need it. Is that true?"

"Sometimes," Zack said.

Rosie was a bit upset to hear Zack agree with her dad. Most of the time she thought her dad was a bit of a moan and looked for things to complain about instead of trying to do anything to help.

"Why don't we get rid of those guys, then?" she asked Zack.

"It's not our business to get rid of them," he said. "We've already stuck our noses far too much into the way their countries are run."

"Have we?" Rosie asked. She wished again that she could read. She was sure it would be much easier to get her head around complicated things if she could just see them on paper. She watched the news on the TV sometimes, but that wasn't the same. They told you what was happening, but they didn't have time to explain all the background.

"Of course we have," said Zack. "First of all we went and took over loads of countries and treated the people who lived there like servants, or animals. And then, once that was finished, or almost finished, we started doing things like slave-trading."

Rosie had heard of slave-trading but she didn't know much about it. At least she didn't have to say so this time, as Zack had got into his stride and it was clear was going to tell her about it whether she wanted him to or not.

"Slave-trading is one of the most evil things that anyone ever did to anyone else in the whole history of the world," Zack said. "And we all have to remember that our country was one of the ones that did it. So that means it was our fault too."

"No, hang on a minute," said Rosie. "That's not fair. OK, it was Britain's fault, but it wasn't *our* fault. We weren't even born then." She stopped and felt her face go red. She had forgotten for a second that she didn't like to argue with Zack in case she came out with something stupid.

Zack looked at her with a frown. "You're right," he said. "We weren't born. But our ancestors were. And they were the ones who bought and sold people like they were animals."

"Yours might have," Rosie said. "Mine didn't. They were all miners. My mum did our family tree with my gran. Our family never had any money. No way they bought anybody."

"Well, they didn't stop other people doing it," Zack said. "The whole country got richer with the money the slave traders made. Our great-great-great grand-parents had nice, comfy lives while the slaves suffered to pay for them."

Rosie couldn't believe what she was hearing. "Yeah, right," she said. "One time, we went to see the place where my family lived. There's a museum there. It was horrible. People spent all their time down in the mine in the dark, from morning to night." She shivered as she remembered it. "Even the children had to go down. Families were big, but they lived in tiny little houses with no baths or running water. They didn't even get to vote for years and years. Women didn't even get to vote till after the First World War. So you can't say that they let people have slaves. They had no say at all!"

"Wow, Rosie," Zack said. "That's about the most words I've heard you say at one go since I got to know you."

"Well," Rosie said, feeling pleased with herself, "if I said stupid things like you do, you wouldn't sit there with your mouth shut and let me, would you?"

Zack smiled. "No," he said. "And it's nice to know you do have opinions. I was starting to think you were going to stay shy of me forever and never say anything at all."

Rosie went red again but then Zack smiled at her and she laughed. He went over and bought them coffee and cakes and they chatted for a while about different things. Then Zack picked up the leaflet again and his face grew sad.

"Imagine what it must have been like for African slaves," he said. "One day they were busy thinking about what to cook for dinner or what to plant in the fields. The next, they were chained up on some ship in the most awful conditions, on the way to a place they had never seen. And when they got there they had no rights, no money, no hope. Just a life of slaving away for rich people who paid them nothing, and all the time they knew it would be the same for their children, and their children's children, and their children's children's children."

"When did it end?" Rosie asked.

"1808," Zack said. "That's when William Wilberforce got slavery made illegal. But that was just in Britain. Lots of other countries kept on doing it for ages."

Rosie took the leaflet from him and looked at it. The words were as much of a blur as usual, but there was a big photo of a little girl at the top. She had smooth brown skin and huge eyes, and she looked very, very ill.

"Her tummy is so swollen," Rosie said. "But her legs are so thin, like little sticks. Why is that?"

"That's what happens when people starve," Zack told her. "She's just a little kid, but she's going to die. That's why we have to help."

All of a sudden Rosie felt sick. She pushed her cake plate away.

"What can we do?" she asked.

"I want to try to raise some money," Zack said. "Will you help me? I thought we could maybe write letters to local shops and see if they would give us prizes for a raffle."

Rosie felt the smile freeze on her face. Write a letter? She would be doing well if she managed to write her own name.

When the café shut Zack said he had to go home to speak to his brother on the phone – he tried to ring every week to speak to the family. Rosie wandered home alone, feeling low and sad. She had hoped that she would be able to learn to read before Zack had found out she couldn't. She had taken the first steps on the road, but there was still so far to go, and now she was going to have to tell him.

There was no one in the house to take Rosie's mind off her problems, so she went upstairs, curled up on the bed and started to cry.

Why did she have to be born so stupid?

Chapter 2
No Place for a Woman

The next thing Rosie knew, it was morning. Her eyes felt puffy from crying and the bright sun made them sore. Her back was as stiff as if she had slept all night on the floor. The room also seemed to be rocking a bit, to and fro. Maybe she had the flu. That was all she needed – then she couldn't even go to her reading group that night!

After a second, Rosie opened her eyes all the way and looked at the room around her. Her stomach flipped over in shock. The walls were made of wood panels and the room was very small – a bit like someone's study, only the window was round and not much bigger than a dinner plate. There was a wooden table with a map on it, and funny instruments that Rosie thought she had seen somewhere before, perhaps in a museum. It was nothing like her bedroom.

Rosie's heart started to beat faster. "Oh no," she said to herself. "I'm in the past again. But where?"

Someone was shouting outside the door – that must have been what had wakened her.

"Rosie! Damn it, lass, are you not up yet?" It was a man's voice, deep and low.

Rosie scrambled to her feet. She had been sleeping in a cotton dress and there was a shawl on the end of the bed. She snatched the shawl and put it on. "I'm up!" she shouted. "I'm coming!"

The voice had come from behind the door to Rosie's right and she hurried over to open it. On the other side was a smaller cabin. There was a man sitting up in a bed by the wall. He was stout, with a neck like a bull and thick, messy grey hair. His face was so tanned that it was almost the same colour as the wood of the floor, but his eyes were a funny greeny-blue.

"Good morning, niece," the man said. "Now be a good lass and fetch me my breakfast." He shook his head as if he was just waking up.

"Yes ... uncle," Rosie said. She turned to go in search of the kitchen and nearly fell as the whole floor rocked again. She must be on board a ship! Did it belong to this man who said he was her uncle?

It was a ship, and it was very small. Outside the door, Rosie had only a few steps to go to reach the little room the cook made the food in. The cook himself was a tiny, thin man with a long nose and a big smile.

"Captain's breakfast?" he said to Rosie. "Here y'are." He passed her a plate with stew on it, and some things that looked like hard biscuits. Then he poured ale into a tin cup and passed that over as well. "What are you waiting for, lass? Get on wi' you."

So Rosie had been right – the man who said he was her uncle was the ship's Captain. She took the plate and cup, trying not to spill them, and made her way back to the cabin with the meal.

Rosie sat with the Captain while he ate and when he had finished, he took her up on deck. She was a bit scared, because he said that not all the men liked having a girl on board. Some of them thought it was bad luck for the ship. Some others were hard, rude men and Rosie would have to be careful to stay well away from them and behave like a proper young lady, as her father would wish. That was why Rosie was on the ship, she had found out – her mother had died and her uncle was taking her to her father in the Indies.

Up on deck, Rosie was amazed to see how small the ship was – not even 60 feet long, and no more than 20 feet across the beam. It was square at the back and had three masts. The tallest one was in the middle and seemed to go up forever, at least 60 feet into the swirling clouds in the sky. As far as Rosie could see in any direction the ocean stretched on without end.

"It's fair weather," a sailor said to her, with a big smile that showed his broken teeth. "There's not a sail in sight."

"Is that good?" Rosie asked, then wished she hadn't. It sounded stupid.

"Of course it's good, lass," the sailor said, with a shake of his head. "No sails means no Frenchmen. And it means no British men-o'-war. And no privateers with their greedy eyes on our cargo."

Rosie tried to look as if she understood, but she had no idea what the man was talking about. Why would they be afraid of the French, even less of the British? They were as British as anyone!

"Now, now," the Captain said to the sailor. "There's no need to scare the lass with talk like that. We'll be quite safe, Rosie, quite safe. Didn't I promise your father I'd bring you to him in the Indies in one piece?"

Just then a look-out up on the mast spotted a sail far to the north. Everyone stopped what they were doing for a moment or two. A young sailor shaded his eyes with his hand and peered at the horizon.

"Is it French?" he said, and there was fear in his voice. "A man-o'-war, d'you think?"

The older man next to him tried to follow his line of sight. He had bow-legs and wind-burn so bad his skin looked like old wood. "We don't want a man-o'-war of any sort," he said, with a grim smile. "One of our own ain't no better. They would take us down like a shot."

The young man looked at him, puzzled.

"Where have you been?" the old sailor asked, pulling his face into a frown. "They passed the damn Bill, didn't they? If we get caught, that's the end of us."

Rosie wanted to ask the man what Bill he was talking about, but she didn't think that her uncle would like her to talk to the men. But what other way could she find out why they were afraid of French and British ships? It was clear that they were British, so that made no sense. Rosie was very worried.

She felt even worse when she saw the guns. They were big cannons and they looked like they could fire balls which would break the timbers of a ship, or bring down the masts with a lucky strike. Were her uncle and his men pirates? The thought chilled her like a bucket of cold water thrown over her whole body.

How far were they from land? Who were they looking to rob, perhaps kill? Her uncle seemed like such a nice man, with such good manners. Why would a man who wanted his niece to behave like a proper young lady choose such an awful way of life? Or was that what all bad people were like – did they have rules for how they behaved among themselves, while they still killed and robbed and attacked strangers?

Chapter 3
Down in the Hold

In the early evening the sun sunk in the west, splashing the waves with red and yellow, like spilled paint the colours of fire. Rosie sat in the Captain's cabin and ate her dinner with her uncle, some other sailors and the ship's doctor. The doctor was a thin, mild-mannered man with bony hands, who had lost one finger on the left. He saw Rosie staring at the stub of it.

"I hardly miss it," the doctor said with a smile. "Most folks lost their heads."

Rosie thought she must have heard him wrong. "What did you say, sir?" she asked.

"Heads, lass," the doctor repeated. He drew his fingers across his throat like a knife. "The Revolution in France. Madame Guillotine cut off their heads till the streets of Paris ran with blood. 1789, that was. Before old Napoleon. Seems like another age now. In fact, I dare say you weren't even born."

"I'm sixteen," Rosie told him, in the hope that the man would work out for her whether she had been born or not in 1789. She still had no idea what year they were in.

The doctor smiled, showing teeth which were much better than Rosie had expected. "You were somewhere near born, then, lass. If it's 1812 now and you're sixteen, you must have been seven when they had the great battle at Trafalgar. That set old Napoleon back a bit." All of a sudden his face was filled with sorrow. "Lost Lord Nelson in that battle, we did. Not much could make up for that. And Napoleon's still master of Europe, damn his hide. But we'll get him yet. Money, that's what a lot of it comes down to – you can't fight a war without money."

Rosie didn't think of that again until the following day when she went below deck to the hold for the first time. She knew her uncle would be angry but a boy had come to his cabin looking for him and Rosie couldn't find him anywhere. After she had checked all the places she could think of above deck, she went below to the cargo hold.

In the hold she discovered what that cargo was. She smelled it and heard the noise before she got there. It wasn't the stink of sea-water and damp, it was more animal than that, more like sweat and dung. The sounds were moans, shouts now and then, and the clink of chains against the rings that held them to the sides of the ship.

Slaves. Dozens and dozens of them, black bodies all jammed in so close there was no room to stand. There was only a five foot gap between one deck and the next. Some of the slaves were big men, tall, and their shoulders were hunched and their backs bent to fit in the tiny space.

Rosie stood frozen to the spot. Her stomach flipped as if she were about to be sick.

Perhaps she made a noise, because just then some of the slaves turned and looked at her. She wanted to look away, ashamed, and yet she couldn't. Now it all made sense. She was on a slave ship, and her uncle was part of that awful trade Zack had told her about. Her uncle bought human beings on the Coast of Africa and took them across the sea to the Indies. There he must sell them and buy sugar to take back to Liverpool or Bristol, or wherever, and buy goods there to begin the first part of the journey over again. There was profit whichever way they sailed – if they survived.

The doctor said that Britain was at war with Napoleon and the French. They could lose. They could be invaded, like the rest of Europe. The great victory of Trafalgar was years ago. No wonder the sailors were scared of seeing a French ship on the horizon.

And a British one? They were scared of that too, because since 1808, slaving was illegal.

And privateers? They would rob them of their cargo.

Did they have a friend anywhere on this enormous sea?

"Get out of there, girl!" a rough voice shouted. "What will the Captain say if he finds out we let you down here?"

Hard hands grabbed Rosie's arms and tried to pull her over to the door.

"The Captain will say worse things if I tell him you put your hands on me!" she said to the sailor who had grabbed her. "Get on with your work! I will go back up in a moment."

The sailor grumbled but he let go of Rosie and picked up the buckets he had with him. The buckets were full of food and water and he gave these to the slaves just like he would put out food and water for animals.

Rosie watched, wanting to see the slaves but not the way the sailor treated them. Many of them were more beautiful than any people she had ever seen.

Then as if he knew he was being watched, and didn't like it, one big man parted his lips and smiled at her. Rosie felt the shock go right through her body and leave her cold. The man's teeth were filed into points, like a wolf's fangs, only worse.

Rosie pushed past the sailor and made her way up into the air. She had to bend down low so as not to crack her head on the deck above her.

"Does my father know you sell slaves?" she asked the Captain as soon as he came back into the cabin. The Captain looked at her for a moment, then he sat down at the table and started to play with his compasses, moving the legs back and forth on a piece of paper with figures written on it.

"He suspects," he said. "I'm not sure he's at all happy to have you on *The Red Rose*, but there was no choice when your mother died."

The Red Rose? Rosie almost choked. It was such a pretty name for such an ugly boat. Her own name, for a slave ship!

"Where do they come from?" she asked.

"There," the Captain answered, and jabbed his finger on the map in front of him. "The West Coast of Africa."

Rosie went round to the same side as the Captain and looked at the map. "Where are we now?" she asked.

The Captain moved his finger several inches into what looked like the middle of the ocean.

"The slaves have got teeth like animals," Rosie said in a hushed voice.

The Captain gave a bark of a laugh. "Some of them," he agreed. "They do that on purpose, to make themselves look fierce. Lot of good it did them."

"Against us, do you mean?" Rosie asked.

"No, lass, against each other," the Captain said. "They are prisoners of war, taken by their own people."

"And they gave them to us?" Rosie found that hard to believe.

"They sold them to us, lass, sold them," the Captain said. "That way they have no more enemies to bother them. If we take them they don't have to feed them or guard them, which they can't afford to do – they have very little food as it is. So they sell them at a good profit."

"And we take them to the Indies and sell them there?" Rosie said.

It was clear the Captain didn't want to give her a proper answer. "At least they're alive," he said. "And we get our money to take back to Liverpool, so we can build more ships to beat Napoleon and the French. The Middle Passage is the worst bit. When we go back home with our sugar an' rum it'll be easier."

Rosie didn't answer. She would not be on the boat on the way home. She would be with her father in the Indies. Her father, who had let them put her on board the Red Rose, with a cargo of slaves.

They were still sitting there, not saying much, when there was a sharp rap on the door.

The Captain looked up. "Come!" he ordered.

The doctor came in and closed the door behind him. He glanced at Rosie, then looked at the Captain. His face was white and there was a tiny muscle twitching under his eye.

"What is it?" the Captain asked.

"Second Mate, sir," the doctor replied.

"Sick? What's wrong with him?"

"Not sick," the doctor said. "He seems to be losing his sight, sir."

"Then do something for him, man! What use is a blind sailor to anyone?"

"That's the trouble, sir," the doctor said. "I don't know that I can."

The Captain shook his head. "Well I suppose that's why we carry three mates. Do what you can for him. He was a good man."

"Yes, sir."

Chapter 4
Going Blind

Several days went by without Rosie really being aware of them passing. There just seemed to be a blur of light and darkness, movement and rocking whether she was awake or asleep. Still they had seen no ship on the horizon, and that at least was something to give thanks for.

Her uncle had kept her shut up in the cabin most of the time, but she had still seen the slaves being let up on the main deck, a few at a time. The sailors tried to get them to dance, even to sing. No one wanted them to grow sick and sad on the journey. They would be worth far less. They were still chained, of course. No risks were taken.

One time Rosie was crossing the deck when she saw a landsman with some slaves. The landsmen weren't sailors – their only job was to look after the slaves. The man was cursing under his breath as the slaves were slow and clumsy as they walked back to their quarters after their turn on deck. The landsman had a long stick which he used to prod them on.

One of the slaves tripped and fell onto his knees.

The landsman froze, thinking perhaps that the slave was trying to trick him, maybe even attack him. It sometimes happened, even among women slaves.

Rosie started to go over to see if the fallen man was alright.

"Watch it!" the landsman shouted. "Don't get too close!"

The slave got to his knees, and then reached out for something to hold onto before he got to his feet. It was then that Rosie saw that his eyes were puffed and bloody and he could not see. She swung around and stared at the rest of the slaves. How many more were blind? There was another one with his hand on the arm of the man in front of him. A third stared round, confused and shivering with fear.

Rosie went over to the landsman. "They're blind," she said. Her voice shook.

"That's rubbish!" The landsman almost choked on the words. "Course they're not. Don't let them fool you."

"Look at them!" Rosie said. "Half of them have gone blind, just like the Second Mate."

"It can't be!" But even as he denied it, Rosie could see that the landsman knew it was true. "We'd have seen," he went on. "You're wrong."

But Rosie was not wrong. Almost a quarter of the slaves were at least partly blind, some in one eye, some in both. Now two of the crew had swollen eyes, too, seeping pus.

The weather grew worse. A hard wind sprang up from the north and the Captain and his men had to work hard not to be blown off course. There always needed to be at least two men on watch for ships on the horizon. Anyone else on the sea could be an enemy, and as they grew closer to the Indies the chances of passing another ship got more and more.

Rosie was waiting in the galley for the Captain's dinner a few nights later when the cook picked up his knife to slice the meat. Rosie was only half watching him as he sliced hard, pressing the knife so it would cut the dry, tough meat.

All of a sudden the cook let out a high, awful scream. Blood was pouring over the meat, fresh, bright and red.

For an instant Rosie froze. Then she remembered all of the awful wounds she had seen in the hospital in Belgium in World War One. This was nothing in comparison.

The cook screamed again, holding his hand up in the air, just four fingers and a scarlet stump. His other arm was waving around as if he wanted to reach for something. His face was screwed up with pain and terror.

Rosie dived for the only clean piece of rag she could see and grabbed it. "Hold still!" she shouted. "Hold still, or you'll bleed to death!" That was maybe a bit dramatic, but it had the effect she wanted. The cook stopped screaming and stood still.

Rosie grabbed his hand, still pouring with blood, and tied the rag around the stump of his finger as tight as she could.

"Sit down," she ordered, then she ran out the door, shouting for the doctor. "Now!" she yelled. "Hurry!"

When Rosie got back the cook was sitting on the floor and his face was grey with shock, but at least the finger was not bleeding so much.

"Hold it up," Rosie ordered, then grabbed his wrist and lifted it. "I know it hurts. I'll get you some rum in a minute, just keep still now."

It was only another moment before the doctor came in. "What happened?" he asked, getting to his knees, wiping his eyes and peering at the shocked cook.

"Cut me finger off," the cook said. "Couldn't see what I was doing."

The doctor got out a bottle of spirit and a needle which he told Rosie to thread for him. Then he lifted up the bloody bandage a bit and saw that the stump was still bleeding, but less than before.

"This is going to hurt," he warned. "But I have to do it."

He took the threaded needle from Rosie, thanked her, then unwound the bandage and tied thread tight round the finger to keep it from bleeding.

As she watched, Rosie's heart filled with a cold horror. She realised that the doctor also could not see, at least not well. That was why he had asked Rosie to thread the needle. Rosie stared at the doctor, her breath tight in her chest. He put the needle in the cook's flesh, almost dropping it once or twice, and at last gathered the skin over the raw bone and pulled it together.

That evening the Captain asked Rosie what had happened. Rosie wanted to lie, to make it less scary than it was, but the truth forced itself out of her mouth, and she knew it was in her eyes anyway. She told the Captain how the cook couldn't see well enough to chop the meat without cutting his own fingers, and that the doctor couldn't see to thread a needle, or even to stitch a wound.

The Captain poured himself a glass of rum and his face was white, the sun and wind burn on it looking yellow, as if there were no blood in his veins. He nodded a time or two and said nothing. With a sudden shock of fear greater than she could remember feeling before, Rosie saw that her uncle also was afraid. They were alone, until they reached harbour. Their cargo was against them, every other ship was against them, and the sea was against them all.

Chapter 5
Who to Trust

During the next few days the weather began to grow worse. A hard wind rose in the west and they had to take down the sail and head north. One of the crew slipped from the mast and fell to the deck. He died where he landed.

For the second man to fall, death was not so fast. The ship rocked far to one side and he landed in the sea, still alive. By then things were so bad that the Captain had let Rosie go anywhere she chose on the ship so she was there to hear him shouting and see him thrashing in the water. Of course there was no way they could bring the ship around in time to go back for him. They were running hard in front of a gale and it might be miles before they could turn back, even if they could find the same spot again in the great stretch of sea. The man would be drowned long before that, even if the sharks hadn't taken him. In this weather the crew couldn't even stop to lower a little boat to go back and get him.

It was a sad crew that came to eat that night, and a poor supper, made by Rosie who had gone to help the cook since he could now not see or use his right hand any more. Worse than that, the doctor was now almost totally blind as well, as were most of the crew. Fear was so strong that Rosie could almost taste it in the air, smell it in the small dark spaces of the ship.

When Rosie went to take the Captain's dinner to him she found him sitting at his table, both hands on the maps, staring at the door.

"Uncle?" Rosie said in a dry whisper.

"Is that you, Rosie?" the Captain asked, his eyes narrowed to try to see.

Rosie shuddered. "Can't you see me?"

"I can see there's someone there." The Captain drew a deep breath. "But I can't see your face." Another deep breath. "Come in and close the door, lass. We've got to do something about this. Can't sail a ship with a blind crew."

Rosie shut the door and waited.

"The First Mate tells me some of the slaves can still see," the Captain told her. "I can't believe I'm even thinking about doing this, but without somebody to help we'll all go down."

"What do you mean?" Rosie asked.

"Come down to the hold with me, lass, and we'll see what we can find. Any man who is still fit can help sail, and any fit woman can do the cooking. You will have to work out who you can trust. See if you can spot four or five ...."

"I don't know who to trust!" Rosie said. "I don't know anything about them! You told me to stay away from the sailors, never mind the slaves!"

"I know," the Captain said. "But it's different now." He spoke more softly. "Look into their eyes, lass. If they won't look back at you, or they can't see you, leave 'em. If they look right at you, try to explain to them what's happened. Try to make them understand we'll all drown if we lose the ship. I'll be with you."

"But I can't ..." Rosie began. "I don't know what language they speak. Perhaps the landsmen can do it ..."

"They can't see any better than I can, lass," said the Captain. "I hate to ask you, Rosie, but you have to do this. You're the only one who can see a face clear enough to see if you can trust the man or not. Now go do it."

"Uncle ..."

"Go do it, lass. You're my eyes now, an' my legs."

Shivering, Rosie stumbled out of the Captain's cabin, all but tripping over the uneven floor. The Captain walked slowly behind her and she kept a few steps ahead. It was an awful thing he had asked her to do. How on earth could she look at those prisoners and tell which of them to trust? They might grab her and break her neck the minute she let them free – her uncle couldn't see to stop them! Or they could do something worse ... Rosie could hardly blame them if they attacked her. She would want to fight, in their place.

And what would she say to them anyway? She couldn't speak their language, and as far as she knew, none of them could speak hers. This was the worst nightmare she could imagine, to be stuck on a ship with a blind crew, enemies all over the seas, and no help but prisoners who had been caged up like wild animals until they could be sold, if they even lived as far as the Indies.

Before she could think up any answers to her questions, Rosie and the Captain were at the hold, looking into the place where the slaves were chained, bent over in the five feet of room. Rosie only needed one look to see that most of them were as blind as the crew. This was probably where it had started. It had only spread because no one ever looked the slaves in the eyes.

How could Rosie tell who could see her? She had not even thought of that until now. She must do something that would make them look. She could bring something to eat that they could find only by sight, not smell.

"Wait here," she said to her uncle, and ran off.

She came back in a few seconds with ships' biscuits. The biscuits were hard and tasteless, and in this place that was so full of other smells, they smelt of nothing. Rosie held one out, raising her hand with it held between her fingers.

No one moved.

Rosie pretended she was going to bite it herself, then offered it again.

A boy about Rosie's age came forward, pushing his way between older men. He was gentle, as if he knew that he could see and they could not. His eyes met Rosie's and he waited.

How on earth could Rosie explain what she wanted? She pointed to the boy's eyes, then to the rest of the prisoners behind him, and shut her own, as if she were blind.

The boy nodded, then held up his fingers, and thumb. Five? Was that what he meant? Could five of the slaves see?

Rosie pointed at the Captain's blind eyes, and then at her wide open ones.

The boy nodded.

Rosie smiled. The boy looked young and scared – she didn't think he would hurt her. She pointed to herself, then up at the deck as if to the rest of the crew, and shut her eyes tight. Then she opened her eyes and looked at the boy's face. He understood. He knew he was a prisoner locked in the hold of a ship manned by a blind crew.

Rosie made the sign for five again, and pointed at her eyes, then waved to show him that she wanted the five who could see to come forward. Then she pointed at the locks of the boy's chains to show she wanted to open them. She mimed cooking, chopping, stirring, climbing ropes, pulling down the sails, then she started all over again.

Again the boy seemed to understand. He went into the crowd of people, and spoke to them in his own language. There was an argument but in the end he won, and he came back with an adult woman, two girls who were a little younger than Rosie, and an old man. Rosie could see right away that their eyes were fine. She was happy with the woman and the two girls, but she was a bit worried about the older man. He had a grey beard and arms and chest with muscles like ropes. His eyes were steady and hard.

Rosie shook her head.

The boy nodded, pointing to the man again. He pointed at his eyes, his chest, and nodded till his head nearly came off.

For a few seconds more Rosie bit her lip, worried, but then she decided that she had nothing to lose. The man was strong. Without him they would never be able to work the ship. Then they would all die.

40

Chapter 6
At Their Mercy

Rosie let the five slaves out, locked the cage behind her and gave the key to the Captain. Blind or not, he would be strong enough to defend himself if he had to. Rosie knew that it would be very easy to take the keys from her if any of the slaves attacked.

The next thing to do was to take the woman to the cook and show her what to do to make food. Rosie didn't want to give her knives, so she showed her the tubs of beans, rice and corn instead. She could cook those and the knives could stay locked up, with the key safe in the Captain's pocket.

The cook moaned about a slave being in charge of the cooking, but the Captain spoke to him and in the end he agreed to leave her there and go and rest.

"Your food is awful anyway," Rosie said with a smile. "I'm sure this woman will do a better job."

The cook smiled, even though he must have been in pain from his hand and eyes. He thought that Rosie had saved him from bleeding to death and there was no one on Earth like her.

With a lot of effort and far more patience than she believed she had, Rosie showed the woman what it was that she was to do. She would have to feed everyone with a set amount of food every day. The prisoners could not leave the hold with no one to watch over them, so food and water would have to be taken to them. And because the crew were all blind, they would have to have their food and water taken to them too.

Rosie had learned from the cook where everything was kept and how to measure it and cook it. After what seemed like ages she felt that the woman understood what to do, with the two girls to assist her. Rosie thought that the woman even wanted to help, so that she and all the other slaves could survive this awful journey.

So tired she could hardly walk, Rosie dragged herself back up onto the deck to begin to explain to the man and the boy what they would have to do. Before that, of course, she would have to learn it all herself. For that she needed the Captain to tell her how to set their course, and the First Mate to tell her how to work the sails. The Captain would be alright, but the First Mate wasn't likely to be very happy to explain these things to a girl.

As Rosie crossed the deck to find the Captain, she found the other free slaves backed up against the base of the mainmast, with the crew all round them, shouting and swearing. All of the crew members were blind, but they knew that some of the prisoners were free and they had linked arms and made a circle around them, closing them in.

Rosie felt the slaves' terror as if it were her own, and also how they must feel that she had tricked them.

"Stop it!" she yelled, hearing the panic in her voice.

"Out of the way, lass!" one of the crew yelled back at her. "There's slaves free!" He turned to the mast. "I'm not as blind as you think, you devils! I'm not going to be murdered by one of you lot! I'll kill you first. Now out o' my way, Rosie. This is no place for a woman."

Rosie gulped and felt her heart beating so hard it all but choked her. "Yes, there are prisoners free," she said, as loud as she could. "Two men and three women. I set them free on the Captain's orders ... "

"Fool!" someone else shouted. "I told you there should never be women on board a ship! She'll kill us all!"

"I'm not a fool!" Rosie said, angry now. "We let them out because they can see! Do you want to climb up the mast next time we need to alter sail? You can't see your hand in front

44

of your face – you'll fall and die! And what about food? How long can you live on raw beans and rice before you starve? So I've got a new crew here to sail the ship, and a woman who will cook for you, and feed you. If you want to fall overboard, or starve, say so now! If you want to live, step away from those slaves!" It was a challenge, and Rosie held her breath while they thought about it. She did not dare take her eyes from the one who seemed to think of himself as their leader. He could see a little, and Rosie couldn't move as he would take that as backing down and he would attack.

In the end the leader was the first to take a step back. "You'd better be right, girl," he said. "If you're wrong, I'll break your neck myself and put you over the side for the sharks. I don't care if the Captain is your uncle."

Rosie laughed, a high-pitched, almost mad sound. "If I'm wrong, you fool, we won't need to go over the side. We'll go down with the ship!" She pointed to the slave man and the boy. "They don't want to drown any more than we do."

There were a lot of moans, but one by one the sailors moved backwards, still holding hands, feeling their way, tripping now and then. Rosie had won, but it was just the beginning of the task.

The work was even harder than Rosie had imagined. The crew wouldn't help at all as they still didn't trust the freed slaves one bit. As the hours and days went by Rosie began to see the many reasons for their fear. Most of all she thought they were afraid because they were blind and the slaves could see. They hated the idea that they were helpless and needed the slaves to do everything, and couldn't even tell if they were doing it right. Then of course there was fear just because the slaves looked different, spoke a different language and had a different way of life. Last, and Rosie began to think worst, was the fear that came from knowing that they had kept the slaves prisoner and treated them so badly, and they now were at the slaves' mercy.

Rosie could not completely forget either that she had been on this boat while the slaves had been treated badly. She could not read the older man's thoughts as he carried out the tasks she set him, tring to explain by miming and doing a little of each job herself.

With the woman and girls it was easier. The girls seemed to like Rosie. The woman understood cooking well enough, so Rosie didn't have to tell her much, just make sure she didn't use up all the food too fast, or set the ship on fire by accident.

The hardest things were to keep order and some kind of spirit in the crew, report to the Captain and struggle to read every instrument they needed. It was lucky Rosie didn't need to write much, as it was all numbers, and she could manage those OK if she took her time.

Rosie was so tired she was happy to sleep with all her clothes on, on the floor in the Captain's room where he thought she would be most safe. She never got to sleep for very long. There was always something to be done. Often she was so tired and confused she felt close to weeping, but she knew everyone's lives depended on her. It was a bit like being back in Miss Edith Cavell's hospital in World War I. It helped Rosie to think of Miss Cavell sometimes. She thought Miss Cavell would be quite proud of all the things Rosie was doing now, if only she could know. Funny to think she hadn't even been born yet, in this time.

Chapter 7

Jimmy

Rosie called the slave boy 'Jimmy', because the name he gave himself sounded like that, but longer and harder to say. They spent a lot of time together because so many of the tasks took the strength of two people. Before anything could be done, Rosie had to be told how to do it by a sailor from the crew, then try to explain it to Jimmy. By this time she had even stopped wearing the dresses and shawls she had had at first on the boat, and had started to wear boys' clothes instead. To be honest, she liked the boys' clothes much more.

Sometimes, when she was so tired her whole body was sore and she could barely stay awake, Rosie would sit on the deck and stare at the stars, and often Jimmy would come and sit beside her. One time Rosie told him about the things that had happened to her before, when she had gone back in time to the Spanish Armada and to World War I. She knew Jimmy didn't understand any of the words, but she thought perhaps he understood the feelings. One time, she cried as she spoke about Jack, the soldier she had met in Belgium, and Nurse Cavell, who had died such a sad and brave death. Jimmy held her hand.

Jimmy talked too. Rosie couldn't even tell when one word ended and the next started, but she heard the feelings in what he said. There would be a sudden sadness, a break in his voice as he tried to hold back tears, and she knew that he was talking about the place he had come from. Then they would each fall silent, sitting side by side like old friends. One time Rosie even fell asleep.

Rosie grew closer to the Captain also. She became his eyes, and also his hands, his legs, and at times his voice. She tried to make the crew understand they had to keep order, to wait in patience. She became the doctor's eyes and hands in helping with the minor wounds from accidents caused by blindness. She also helped to make the men believe the doctor's promise that the blindness would pass in the end, to some degree.

"Yeah?" one of the men said, and his voice was bitter. "What the hell use is a half blind sailor, eh? I'll be hanging around the docks begging for the rest of my life. That's if I get back home at all! Where are we? Does anybody know? What if we cross the path of a French ship? We can't even load a gun, let alone fire it!"

"Or a privateer!" another added. "They'll take our stores and what slaves are still fit to sell, and then they'll sink us."

"Even one of our own ships," a third one said. "Slaving's against the law, now."

"Nobody knows we're blind!" Rosie snapped at him. "I saw a ship on the horizon yesterday. They just kept on going. Probably up to no good just like us. Why would they want to attack us?"

"To take our cargo, stupid," the first man said. "And our rations, and water."

"And they don't think we'll fight?" Rosie said, making it clear she thought the man was stupid, not her. "One good shot with guns like ours and we could break their mast and leave them stuck. Or put a hole in the ship, and maybe kill some of their cargo."

"The girl's right," a new voice cut in. "Shut up and stop whining."

Another week passed, and if Rosie and the mate had worked it out right, they were about eight days from port. That was when they first saw the other ship, this time making right for them.

Rosie scrambled down the steps to the Captain's cabin and burst in.

"A ship, bigger than we are," she said, between gasps. "Coming straight at us. I think it's British."

The Captain's voice was tight with fear. "Is it a man-o'-war, Rosie? A privateer, or another slaver? What is it? Tell me what it looks like."

He clambered to his feet. "Help me up on deck. Hurry!"

They panicked and fumbled, slipped and banged as Rosie tried to guide the blind Captain along the narrow corridor and up the steps to the deck. She had to keep her own feet and try to stop the Captain from going too fast, so that everyone would think he was still alright and still in charge. Perhaps it was pointless because so few could see him anyway. But Rosie did not want to let him know that she had seen how weak he had become, how close he was to losing command.

The other ship was near enough that they could see it well. It was going at high speed, all sails up and signal flags flying. Rosie told the Captain.

"It's going to pass too close to us," she said nervously.

Word had spread. There were a dozen of the crew on deck now, the First Mate and the doctor among them, peering into the wind, trying to see something. There was no point in telling them that they were looking about a mile in the wrong direction.

"They've got signal flags up, uncle," Rosie told the Captain. "But I don't know what they mean."

"Describe them to me, Rosie!" the Captain said. "Hurry!"

Rosie took the Captain's telescope and one by one she told him the flags she could see. They waited, their faces keen, and at last hopeful.

"Captain?" Rosie said, swallowing hard.

The Captain's skin was grey. "Sweet Mary, Mother of God," he said, almost under his breath. "They're asking us for help. They're blind."

For a few seconds Rosie could not understand what he had said. Then very slowly it sank in. The other ship had enough men who could see to run up a signal, but no more than that. Rosie didn't even know how to signal, and there was no one but herself and Jimmy to climb the rigging and run the flags up. By the time they had done that, the ship would be too far past them for it to matter. The two ships could do nothing for each other.

They all stood silent as the other ship passed across their starboard bow, probably with no idea how close they were. They watched as it ploughed through the waves, on towards the far horizon.

Chapter 8
A Terrible End

A week later they were within two days of land. The weather was calmer and they were making good speed. Many of the men, both slaves and crew, had got at least some of their sight back, and had hopes that it would get even better. The doctor could see well enough to treat most things, even though he needed Rosie to thread a needle for him, and spell out the letters of some of the labels. He didn't seem to think it was at all odd that she couldn't read. After a while Rosie realised that lots of girls couldn't read in this time. The doctor even started to give her lessons about how the letters fitted together to make sounds and the sounds to make words.

The Captain could not thank Rosie enough. He gave her a gold watch with blue and pink enamel flowers and told her it had been his wife's but she had died.

"You saved the ship, Rosie," he said, with feeling. "And every man on it. I'll never listen to another man who says women are bad luck on a ship."

"Thank you, Uncle," Rosie replied, feeling pride fill her heart. Now she knew a bit of what Edith Cavell had felt when she had saved soldiers' lives, risking her own all the while. Or what Queen Elizabeth had felt when she had stood strong against the Spanish Armada.

"Women can do more than you think," she said.

The Captain smiled and slapped her on the back. "It seems they can, Rosie. It seems they can."

Rosie held the watch tight in her hand. It was very warm and the heat seemed to travel all the way up her arm and into her heart.

The warm feeling did not last. That evening was the worst of Rosie's entire life. Many of the slaves were still blind or could see only a little. It had not been possible to have them up on deck for any exercise or fresh air, because there had been no one to guard them. Now they were weak and many were ill. The doctor and the First Mate had to sort them into those who were fit and worth selling, and those who were not.

Rosie ran on to the deck when she heard the screaming but she was too late to stop what was happening. All of the slaves who were of no value any more had been chained together and thrown over the side into the sea to drown in the water. The screaming came when the sharks took them and the clear blue water turned dark with blood.

Rosie was sick with horror. She had never imagined anything so fearful, such terror and pain. She screamed. She threw herself at the crew and had to be held back by force. Hands like the grip of a vice held her arms to her sides. She screamed until she lost her voice, choking, tears running down her face, and it all made no difference at all.

When at last they let her go she was sick, bent over on her hands and knees on the deck, heaving up her guts. When there was nothing left to throw up she went cold, sick and sore. She was so burned up with shame that she could not even look at the faces of the slaves who were still alive. Above all, she could not bear to look and see if Jimmy was there.

Early the next day Rosie went to the Captain, as usual, but this time it was not to take his breakfast, or sit with him and talk about the weather and the sea. Her teeth were locked tight and her whole body shook. Her stomach was burning with fear.

"Where's my breakfast, lass?" the Captain asked, in a kind voice. "Don't worry about yesterday – the men understand why you carried on the way you did. I should never have let you see what happened. We can't sell sick slaves but still no one likes getting rid of them, not even the men. I'm sorry you saw it, but now you must stop thinking about it, Rosie. Go and get my breakfast, there's a good lass."

"No," Rosie said. "I have to make sure you aren't going to sell Jimmy and the other slaves who helped us. I just need to know."

"Of course I'm going to sell them," the Captain said, his eyes wide in shock at the question. "They're the best we've got. And that young lad's smart and strong. He's worth more than most. Top price, I imagine."

Rosie swallowed hard. Her lip hurt and it took a minute to realise she was biting it.

"You can't," she said. "They saved the lives of the whole crew. Without them you'd be shark food yourself."

"Don't worry about Jimmy, lass," the Captain said. "His owners will treat him alright. They'll pay a lot for him, so they won't hurt him."

Rosie shut her eyes. "He and the others saved your life. Is this how you repay them? Sell them to the highest bidder? Is that how white men say 'thank you'?"

"He's a slave," the Captain said softly. "That's what he's for, Rosie."

"Well then, you can sell me too," Rosie said.

"Don't talk rot!" the Captain said. "What's the matter with you, lass?"

"Jimmy worked night and day by my side," Rosie said. "He saved the crew's lives, and yours. You can't sell him. It's … it's a filthy thing to do. How could anyone look you in the face again after that?" She put the watch down on the table in front of him. "I couldn't," she said, "and I don't think your wife would have been able to either."

The Captain's face went white with shock and he put his hand to his chest as if Rosie had hit him there.

"Please!" Rosie said. "Please don't sell them! You can't! You just can't!" She struggled against the catch in her voice and the tears on her face – she didn't want him to think she was just a silly foolish girl. "I'd sooner be dead than live standing by and seeing you do that," she said. She meant it. It would hurt for the rest of her life.

The Captain was silent for what seemed like ages. Then he let out his breath in a long sigh. "What do you want me to do?" he asked.

"I don't know."

"I suppose I could keep them on the ship till we get home to England," he said. "They'd be free then."

"Would they?" Rosie asked. "Are you sure?"

"Oh, yes," the Captain said. "It's happened before. The King said there would be no slaves in England. Would that do you, lass? I suppose I do owe them something."

Rosie felt tears run down her face. She tried to smile.

The Captain picked up the watch and held it out to Rosie.

"Take it," he said. After a second, Rosie did.

"Yes, Uncle," she said. "Thank you."

Chapter 9
Home Again

Rosie landed with the Captain and some of the crew. She saw the harbour at Kingston, the buildings, the green trees, the people in the streets, and the slave market. She saw the slaves stand there in chains, silent, and naked while people looked at them, argued over them and bid for them.

She saw the slaves who had already been here for years, going about their work. They kept their eyes down, would not look up to meet a white man's gaze.

When Rosie went to sleep that night on the boat, she knew she would wake up in the morning in her own time. This journey to the past hadn't been like the times she had come back before.

The first time, she had been lost and confused. She had tried to help someone but it had turned out that her help wasn't needed so she hadn't really done anything at all.

The second time she had found it easier to cope with all the different things and had done more but she had woken up in her own time before she had a chance to really make a difference.

This time she had actually done something, saved five people from the life of hell they would have lived if it hadn't been for her. And now she had a good idea of how she could help more people, too.

So the next morning she was not surprised to wake up in her own bed, with the blue and pink enamel watch held tightly in her hand. It was Saturday – no need to go to school and plenty of time to carry out her plan.

The little antique shop in the High Street was closed more often than it was open but somehow Rosie knew that the owner would be there today. She hung about until it was ten o' clock and then knocked on the dusty glass of the door.

After a moment the door opened and a face peered out. It was long and lean, with a strong nose, but it was very gentle. Even so it was the man's eyes that held Rosie so she could not look away. They were clear and blue, as if he could see inside her. Rosie had met him only three times before, but he was as familiar as if she had known him all her life.

"Rosie," the man said. "I thought it might be you."

Rosie walked into the shop and put the watch down on the counter. The man picked up a magnifying lens and held the watch up to the light to look at it.

"A lovely thing," he said. "But it speaks to me of sadness. I think it has seen many awful things in its time. Am I right?"

"Yes," Rosie said, shivering as she remembered the screams of the slaves in the shark-filled water.

The man put the watch down on the counter and looked at Rosie.

"Would you like to tell me about it?" he asked.

Rosie shook her head. "I think I would like you to tell me about your watches," she said. "They are very special, aren't they?'

"Yes," the man said. "And very powerful, if they are put into the right hands." He smiled at Rosie. "I would like to have this one," he said. "To keep it safe. Will you sell it to me?"

"I came to ask you to sell it for me," Rosie said. "My friend is collecting money for a charity in Africa. I thought I could give him the money it raised."

"A lovely idea," the man said. "But I would rather keep this one safe. So how about I give you another one to sell in its place? One which is not so … special?"

"That's very kind," Rosie said. "But you already gave me a watch – the silver one that was Edith Cavell's. I can't take another from you."

"That watch was meant for you," the man said. "I was just keeping it safe until you came. And I am more grateful to you than I can ever say, for finding this one for me." He picked the watch up again and slipped it into a velvet bag.

"What are they?" Rosie asked. "Are they like keys?"

"That's a good way to put it," the man said. "They can open up time for some people. They lead us to places where people are in need."

"But I didn't have one when I went back this time," Rosie said. "I found it when I was already there."

"That's how it works," the man said. "You can travel back in time towards a watch even if you don't have it with you in your own time. But you can't travel forward without one. If you can't find the watch in the time you travel to, you're stuck there. That's the biggest danger."

"That, and getting shot or killed," Rosie said, remembering the German soldier with a gun who had marched her off in Edith Cavell's hospital.

"The watches are good," the man said. "They protect you. But they're so small. If they don't come to you, like they have all come to you so far, they can be very hard to find. I've spent my life looking for them, all through the world, and all through time."

"Let me help you," Rosie said. "Let me look too."

The man looked at Rosie for what felt like a very long time, his clear blue eyes seeming to see past her face and right into her soul. After several minutes he nodded and smiled.

"Yes," he said. "I think I would like that very much." He moved off into the shop, speaking as he went. "But let's find you a watch to sell first. You mustn't let your friend down."

No, Rosie thought to herself. *I must not let Zack down, or Jimmy, or Jack or Queen Elizabeth or Miss Cavell. I'm not alone any more, and I'm not going to stand by and see terrible things happen to good people. I am going to make a difference.*

Rosie smiled and followed the man into the shop. As she passed, a thousand watches ticked from the cases around her. Keeping time.

Find out what happens next in...

Rose Between Two Thorns

See how it all began...

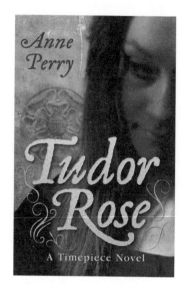

Tudor Rose

2011. Rosie Sands knows she's making the wrong choices in life, but it's tough when you're 15 and you can't even read.

1588. Elizabeth Tudor must face the enemy fleet gathering in the English Channel, but she knows there is danger on every side.

When Rosie finds a very special watch in her school-bag, four hundred years of history disappear to bring her face to face with Elizabeth I. A great Queen and a troubled school-girl find they can help each other in ways no one could have imagined.

Rose of No Man's Land

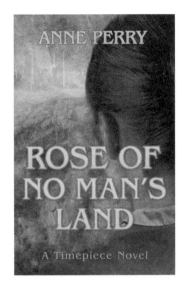

2011. Rosie Sands can't trust anyone enough to admit she has a problem. Not her parents, or her teachers, and especially not Zack Edwards, the coolest boy in school.

1915. Nurse Edith Cavell must put her own life in danger as she helps British soldiers to escape from Belgium under the noses of the Germans. Every day could be her last.

When Rosie is given a WWI nurse's watch and wakes up in Edith Cavell's hospital, she finds herself surrounded by secrets and lies. Does she dare to get involved, or is it easier to look the other way?

Our books are tested
for children and young people by
children and young people.

Thanks to everyone who consulted on
a manuscript for their time and effort in
helping us to make our books better
for our readers.